For Aidan
On your First Halloween
Halloween! Happy Halloween
From Mom & D
We lo

Halloween 2009

SPOOKY STORIES

SPOOKY STORIES

 publications international, ltd.

TABLE OF
CONTENTS

LITTLE ORPHANT ANNIE

From the original poem by James Whitcomb Riley

Little Orphant Annie's come to our house to stay,

And wash the cups and saucers up, and brush the crumbs away,

And shoo the chickens off the porch, and dust the hearth, and sweep,

And make the fire, and bake the bread, and earn her board-and-keep;

And all us other children, when the supper-things is done,

We sit around the kitchen fire and have the mostest fun,

A-listenin' to the spooky tales that Annie tells about,

And the gobble-uns that will get you

IF YOU
DON'T
WATCH
OUT!

THE CANTERVILLE GHOST

Based on the original story by Oscar Wilde
Adapted by Renee Deshommes
Illustrated by Stacy Schuett

The Otis family moved to a grand old house in England called Canterville Chase. When they arrived, they noticed a dull red stain on the carpet in the library.

The old housekeeper smiled. "That bloodstain cannot be removed. It is the blood of Lady Eleanor. Her husband, Sir Simon, still haunts this house."

"That's nonsense!" cried Washington Otis, the eldest son. "Pinkerton's Champion Stain Remover will clean it up in no time."

He scrubbed until the stain was gone.

The next morning, Mr. Otis and Washington found the bloodstain in the library again.

"I don't think it is the Champion Stain Remover that is to blame," said Washington. "It must be the ghost."

One night, Mr. Otis was awakened by a curious noise outside his room. It sounded like the clank of metal. Mr. Otis opened the door and found a ghostly old man.

"Please, sir," said Mr. Otis, holding up a bottle. "Oil your chains with this Rising Sun Lubricator. I must get some sleep."

The ghost angrily threw down the bottle and disappeared through the wall.

The Canterville Ghost went to his secret chamber and thought about his revenge.

The next night, just after the family had gone to bed, they heard a fearful crash in the hall. Mrs. Otis rushed downstairs. There she found the Canterville Ghost sitting next to a suit of armor scattered across the floor. The twin boys aimed their slingshots and each of them fired a shot at the poor ghost.

Just then, Mrs. Otis leaned over and offered some medicine to the ghost. "You are far from well," she said. "I have brought you a bottle of Dr. Dobell's Soothing Remedy."

The ghost glared at Mrs. Otis. With a groan, he vanished into thin air.

The humiliated ghost resolved to try again. The next night, the ghost set out down the hallway. Suddenly, he wailed in terror. Right in front of him stood a horrible ghost. The Canterville Ghost had never seen another ghost before. He was very frightened. He ran back to his room and hid under his blankets.

As the sun came up, the ghost gained some courage. He tiptoed down the hallway. But the other ghost no longer looked frightening. Its head was only a pumpkin and its body was just a white sheet. A sign said "YE OTIS GHOST."

The Canterville Ghost had been tricked!

A few days later, Virginia Otis saw the Canterville Ghost sitting by the window. He looked very sad. Virginia felt sorry for him.

"I have not slept for three hundred years," the ghost said sadly. "I wish to fall asleep and never wake." The ghost needed Virginia's pure heart. If she would be his true friend, the ghost could sleep forever.

Virginia considered the ghost's request. "I will help you," she said. She took the ghost's hand and followed him through the wall.

About ten minutes later, the bell rang for tea. Mr. and Mrs. Otis were greatly alarmed when Virginia did not appear. They searched everywhere for her, but could not find her.

At midnight, Virginia returned from the hidden chamber looking very pale and tired. She was holding a small box.

"Where have you been?" asked Mr. Otis.

"With the ghost. He's gone now," replied Virginia. She showed her family the secret room. She explained that Sir Simon had been locked in this room long ago.

The Otis family had a proper funeral for Sir Simon. Then Virginia remembered the box the ghost had given her.

Virginia opened the box and gasped. "Look at those beautiful jewels," she cried.

The jewels were a gift from Sir Simon, who could finally rest in peace.

KING OF CATS

Adapted by Suzanne Lieurance
Illustrated by Kallen Godsey

The grave digger's wife sat by the fireplace mending socks. Her lazy black cat slept on the floor next to her. It was very late. The woman was waiting for her husband, the grave digger, to come home.

The grave digger's wife and the lazy black cat waited and waited. At last, the grave digger rushed into the house. His face was pale and his eyes were wide.

"You look strange," said his wife. "Did something happen?"

The grave digger could barely speak.

The grave digger's wife stared at him. The lazy black cat stared at him, too.

"I was digging old Mr. Ford's grave," said the grave digger. "I guess I fell asleep. I woke up when I heard a cat say, 'MEOW!'"

"Meow!" said the wife's lazy black cat.

The grave digger's eyes widened even more. He pointed to the cat.

"Yes, just like that!" said the grave digger. "I was very deep in the grave. I looked up over the top of it. I saw nine black cats carrying a coffin," said the grave digger.

"A coffin?" his wife gasped.

"The coffin was covered with a black cloth," said the grave digger.

23

"The cats came closer and closer," said the grave digger. "They said 'MEOW!'"

"Meow!" said the wife's lazy black cat.

"Yes, just like that!" said the grave digger. "Their eyes were shining like little lights. They were looking straight at me, just like your cat is looking at me now." The grave digger backed up and shivered.

"Never mind my cat," said the wife. "What happened next?"

"The cat standing in front of the coffin came closer and closer," said the grave digger. "Finally we were nose to nose!"

"Oh my!" said the grave digger's wife. "Then what happened?"

"The cat spoke to me!" said the grave digger. "He said, 'Tell Old Tom that Old Tim is dead.'"

Then the wife's lazy black cat jumped up.

The grave digger's wife screamed.

The lazy black cat stretched and stretched. He grew taller and taller. Soon he was three times his normal size.

At last, the lazy black cat spoke. "Old Tim is dead? Well, I'm Old Tom. Now I am the King of Cats!"

And with that, Old Tom rushed up the chimney.

The grave digger and his wife never saw the lazy black cat again.

THE MYSTERY ON THE SARGASSO

Written by Lynne Suesse
Illustrated by Jan Gregg-Kelm

John Fields was stranded on a tiny island in the middle of the Sargasso Sea. He had been there for an entire week, ever since a terrible storm had wrecked his small sailboat.

John kept busy by fishing and collecting coconuts. Most of the time, though, John sat and looked out at the blue water.

One day, John saw a dot on the water. The dot was a ship! John could see that it was getting closer. He yelled and waved his arms. He would be saved!

Soon the ship was near the shore. A crew member rowed a lifeboat to John's island.

"I'm happy to see you," John said to the man in the boat. John climbed in and the man rowed back to the ship.

Aboard the ship, the captain and crew welcomed John. "You are a very lucky man," said the captain. He shook John's hand.

John thanked the captain over and over. He knew that he was very lucky. As he looked around the ship, though, John noticed that things seemed strange. The captain and crew were wearing unusual uniforms. They were Americans, like John, but he felt that they were very different.

"Welcome aboard *The Lily Belle*," said a crew member, as he led John into a ballroom. The crew member showed John a table covered with food. "Enjoy! Eat as much as you like," he said.

John could not believe how hungry he was! He bit into a piece of chicken and looked around at all the people in the room.

Suddenly, he realized why these people seemed strange to him. It looked like they were having a costume party!

"Your costume is wonderful," said John to a smiling young woman.

The woman looked hurt. "I'm not wearing a costume. This is my favorite dress."

John felt bad. He didn't know what to say. He excused himself and went to get a drink.

John got a glass of soda from the bartender and looked at a newspaper. The newspaper's date said June 2, 1937!

"You guys got props and everything," John said to a man next to him.

"Excuse me?" said the man.

Just then, John heard the bartender's radio. He heard the man on the radio talk about President Franklin Roosevelt. John could not believe his ears! "What year is it?" John asked the stranger.

"It's 1937," said the man.

John ran out onto the ship's deck.

John knew that something was wrong. "Can you please tell me who the President of the United States is?" he asked a man.

The man laughed, but he answered John's question. "Roosevelt is the president."

John knew that he had to leave the ship. He launched one of the ship's lifeboats and rowed away as fast as he could.

Days later, John was picked up by an American fishing boat. He told the fishermen about the strange ship named *The Lily Belle*.

The fishermen looked at each other in silence. Finally, one of the fishermen said, "That cruise ship disappeared in the Bermuda Triangle almost seventy years ago!"

THE BERMUDA TRIANGLE

Written by Brian Conway
Illustrated by Doug Roy

A long time ago, a sailboat set sail from
Florida with twenty-five sailors aboard. Soon
a storm began to gather. One of the sailors
used the radio to ask a large navy ship for
help. Then the radio stopped working.

A young naval officer heard the sailor's
message. He tried to use radar to find the
sailboat, but it had completely disappeared.

Five years later, the same naval officer
found the sailboat drifting near Florida.
He did not find any people on board, but it
looked like people had recently been there.

Steam rose from a warm cup of coffee on a countertop near the stove. A board game was neatly set up on a table. But the twenty-five sailors have never been found.

Just southeast of the United States is an area called the Bermuda Triangle. It is in the Atlantic Ocean between Miami, Puerto Rico, and the Bermuda Islands. Many sailors and airplane pilots try to stay far away from the Bermuda Triangle. They report that unusual, unexplained things happen in that area.

Their compasses spin wildly in the Bermuda Triangle. Clocks display jumbled numbers. Strange lightning storms are yet another reason sailors and pilots stay away.

Some researchers say more than a hundred ships and planes have disappeared in the Bermuda Triangle. One minute they are there, and the next minute they are gone without a trace.

For years, scientists have been trying to figure out what is so dangerous about the Bermuda Triangle. One answer might be the bad weather. Hurricanes are common there. Other experts think there might be unusual magnetic energy in the Bermuda Triangle.

Some of the most experienced sailors and pilots are afraid of the Bermuda Triangle. They think the dangers of the region can never be explained.

THE LEGEND OF SLEEPY HOLLOW

Based on the original story by Washington Irving
Adapted by Rebecca Grazulis
Illustrated by Jeffrey Ebbeler

In a valley by the Hudson River, there was a town called Sleepy Hollow. There were many tales of strange happenings in this town. Some people said the town was haunted by the Headless Horseman.

One of those people was Ichabod Crane, a sweet-tempered teacher. Ichabod's students could not help but think that their teacher's arms and legs were just a bit too long for his body. In fact, he looked like a scarecrow.

One of Ichabod's favorite things to do was stretch out next to the river and read spooky stories. The only thing that Ichabod loved more than a scary story was a young lady named Katrina Van Tassel.

Katrina was one of Ichabod's music students and she was known throughout Sleepy Hollow for her beauty.

The beautiful Katrina had attracted the attention of a man named Brom Bones. Although Brom was rich and handsome, Ichabod would not give up.

Ichabod went about courting the lovely Katrina, visiting her home and taking her for long walks in the moonlight.

Brom became jealous when he found out that Ichabod was also seeing Katrina. Brom began playing practical jokes. He tried to make Ichabod look silly in front of Katrina.

One autumn afternoon, a messenger arrived at Ichabod's schoolhouse to give him an invitation to a party to be held that night at the Van Tassels'.

Ichabod knew that this was his chance to sweep Katrina off her feet. "She will forget she ever met Brom Bones!" he exclaimed.

As soon as school was over, Ichabod groomed himself for the big event. He combed his hair and studied his reflection in a mirror that hung in the schoolhouse.

Ichabod proudly mounted his horse like a knight in search of adventure. But he was far from being a brave knight. And the horse he rode was not even his own. It was an old plow horse that he had borrowed.

Ichabod was confident when he walked into the party. But his shoulders dropped a bit when he saw his rival, Brom Bones. Ichabod sighed. Would Katrina really choose him over Brom?

"May I have the honor of this dance?" Ichabod asked Katrina quickly.

Soon they were whirling across the floor. Katrina smiled happily, but Brom stood in the corner, jealously watching Ichabod.

Before Ichabod left the party, he heard some people talking about the Headless Horseman. The ghost had been spotted recently. Even though Ichabod loved spooky stories, he began to feel nervous.

It was almost midnight when Ichabod left. There was hardly a sound except for the chirp of the crickets. His heart was beating loudly. He began to whistle to keep his spirits up. Suddenly, Ichabod jumped in his saddle.

"A ghost!" yelped Ichabod.

Then he realized that it was only a tree, white where it had been struck by lightning. But soon he began to hear a thumping noise coming from behind him.

When Ichabod turned around to look, he screamed in horror. The Headless Horseman was about to throw his head! Ichabod dodged, but it was too late. He fell off his horse and the Headless Horseman rode off.

The next morning, a search party found Ichabod's horse. And a little ways from his horse, they found a shattered pumpkin.

Ichabod never came back to Sleepy Hollow. When the townspeople told the story, Brom Bones always had a smile on his face. Was it just Brom throwing a pumpkin or did Ichabod really see the Headless Horseman? No one knows for sure. It has become one of the many mysteries of Sleepy Hollow.

WHITE DOG

Written by Renee Deshommes
Illustrated by Brian Floca

Once there was a boy who had a white dog named Ghost. Joey and Ghost were best friends. They loved to roam the countryside looking for adventure.

One day when they were exploring the woods, Ghost started barking at Joey.

"What's wrong, boy?" asked Joey.

Ghost kept barking until Joey backed away. Then Joey saw a black snake coiled up behind a rock! Ghost had protected Joey.

"What a good boy!" Joey said as they walked back home to the farm.

The next morning, Joey whistled for Ghost. But Ghost did not come.

"Son, I found Ghost this morning," his father said. "He wasn't moving. There was nothing we could do. Ghost was very old."

Joey was heartbroken. He knew he would miss his friend very much.

After Ghost was gone, Joey spent most of his time alone. He explored the woods the way he used to with Ghost.

One day when Joey was walking along the edge of a ravine, he suddenly lost his footing. He fell and landed on a ledge below. Joey's leg was twisted and scraped. He could not climb out of the ravine.

Joey yelled for help. But no one was close enough to hear him.

A few miles down the road, Farmer Green was working in his field. He noticed a white dog running toward him. It looked like Joey's dog.

The dog barked and barked at Farmer Green. "Hey Ghost, how're you doing?" he said. "Haven't seen you in a while."

The dog grabbed the man's trousers in his mouth and tried to pull him along.

"Whoa! Okay!" said Farmer Green. "I'm coming. Let's go."

Farmer Green followed the persistent dog through miles of thick brush and tall trees.

When they came closer to the ravine, the dog disappeared in the brush.

Just then, Farmer Green heard someone crying for help.

Joey looked up and saw Farmer Green standing at the edge of the ravine. "My leg is hurt," Joey yelled.

"Hang on," said the farmer. Farmer Green found a strong vine. He held one end of the vine. Then he threw the other end to Joey.

"Use this to pull yourself up," he said.

Joey grabbed onto the vine. Using his good leg, Joey pulled himself up the side of the ravine. Near the top, Farmer Green reached over and pulled Joey onto the rocks.

Farmer Green found a strong branch for Joey to use as a cane.

"Thank you," said Joey.

Joey stood up and steadied himself with the cane. Farmer Green held onto his other arm. They hiked home through the woods.

"You'd still be sitting in that ravine if your white dog didn't show me where you were," said Farmer Green. "He came to my field and barked and barked. Then he led me out into the woods to find you."

Joey could not believe what Farmer Green was saying. "That couldn't have been my dog, sir," whispered the boy. "My dog died almost a month ago."

A DAY AT VERSAILLES

Written by Suzanne Lieurance
Illustrated by Jane Chambless Wright

In the summer of 1901, Anne and Eleanor traveled to France. The two friends wanted to see the grand palace at Versailles. This palace was Queen Marie Antoinette's home in the late 1700's.

As Anne and Eleanor toured the palace gardens, they noticed an old plow on the side of the road. Then they saw two men dressed as soldiers from the French Revolution.

Even though the gardens were beautiful, Anne and Eleanor felt very gloomy.

The women continued walking through the gardens. It was not long before they found a beautiful gazebo. On a normal day, the gazebo would have been lovely. Yet this did not seem like a normal day. The countryside looked eerie. Anne and Eleanor felt even sadder than before. The trees were still. The birds were silent.

Suddenly, a man rushed up from behind them. He had a peculiar smile. The side of his face was scarred.

The man pointed to a small bridge. He told the women to go across it. Anne and Eleanor crossed the bridge. When they looked back, the strange man was gone.

On the other side of the bridge, Anne noticed a beautiful lady. The lady was sketching the countryside. She was wearing an old-fashioned dress and a pale yellow scarf around her neck. She looked very sad.

Anne shivered as she looked at this elegant lady. There was something familiar about her. But who could she be?

Both of the women could sense the feelings of sadness and gloom growing stronger and stronger. But they could not explain what made them feel so sad.

Anne and Eleanor continued their tour. Soon everything seemed normal again. Nothing else unusual happened that day.

The next year, Anne returned to the French palace. But everything in the palace gardens looked different.

"Where is the plow?" Anne asked. "The bridge is gone, too."

Anne told a gardener about the men in green coats and the man with the scarred face. Then she described the lady sketching.

The gardener explained that all of the things she had seen were from the year 1789.

Anne knew she had stumbled into Marie Antoinette's own sad memory. It was her memory of a day in 1789. She had just learned that an angry mob from Paris was marching toward the palace gates to get her.

YETI

Written by Brian Conway
Illustrated by Jason Wolff

A Sherpa boy named Ang Chiki lived near the mountains of Nepal. His uncle taught him how to hike in the Himalaya Mountains.

One day when he was hiking, Ang saw fresh tracks that crossed the trail. These footprints were large and wide.

Ang put his boot in one. The tracks were deep. They held his feet well. Ang stretched his legs to step in them, one by one.

The tracks stopped at the opening of a dark, icy cave. Ang stepped closer and peeked into the cave. It smelled awful!

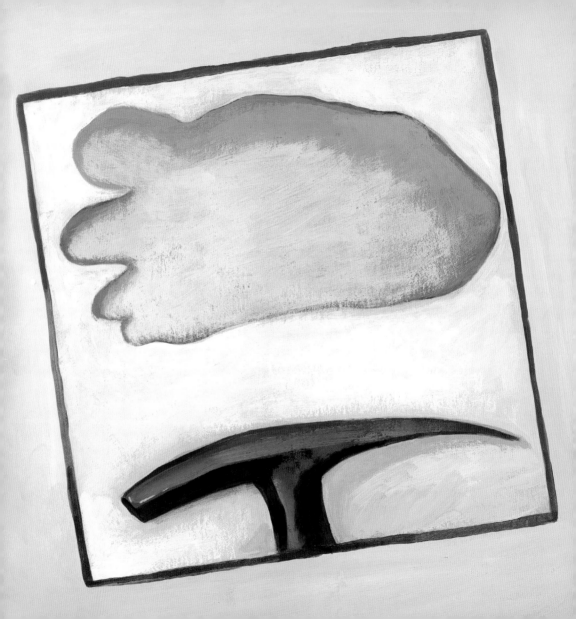

From inside the cave, something grunted and growled. Ang stepped back in fright. His face became as pale and cold as the icy cliffs around him. Ang turned and ran.

The people of Nepal tell stories about wild creatures in the mountains. The Sherpa call them Yeti, which means "snowman." Some people know the Yeti as the "Abominable Snowman."

Many hikers say they have seen these savage snowmen in the mountains of Nepal, Tibet, China, and Russia. They find huge footprints in the snow.

In 1986, a mountain climber claimed he came within thirty feet of a Yeti.

Scientists have searched caves and rocks in the Himalaya Mountains. They only discovered clumps of rough white hairs.

One Sherpa guide has said the Yeti are not real. They are only in the scary stories people tell their children.

Some researchers compare stories of the Yeti with stories about Bigfoot. But Yeti are smaller, and they have white hair. The researchers say the Yeti could be something like a cold-weather cousin of Bigfoot.

In dense jungles, deep oceans, and high moutaintops where few people ever go, scientists are discovering many unfamiliar creatures. Will they ever find a Yeti?

THE MONKEY'S PAW

Based on the original story by W. W. Jacobs
Adapted by Lisa Harkrader
Illustrated by John Kanzler

Mr. White led his old friend Sergeant Major Morris into the parlor. There Mr. White's wife and their grown son, Herbert, sat before a crackling fire drinking tea.

"It's so safe and warm here," said Morris. "I can almost forget that the mysterious jungles of India lurk right outside the door."

"Has something happened to you, Morris?" asked Mr. White.

Morris rubbed his hand across his chin. "My life has nearly been destroyed by a monkey's paw."

Morris reached into his pocket and pulled out a tiny, shriveled hand, covered in fur.

"This small monkey paw has a spell on it," said Morris. "It grants three wishes to anyone who owns it."

"It's magic!" cried Mrs. White.

"It's cursed," Morris said. "Whenever we make a wish, greed clouds our judgment."

"I wouldn't let greed cloud my judgment," said Herbert.

"I thought I was smarter than the monkey's paw," Morris said. "I was wrong. And if I had a fourth wish, I'd wish with all my heart I'd never seen this paw." Then Morris flung the monkey's paw into the fire.

Herbert quickly grabbed a fire iron and fished the monkey's paw from the flames.

"I can't watch you ruin your happy home." Morris rose to his feet. Mr. White walked Morris to the door.

When Mr. White returned, he said, "Morris was right. I live in a fine house with a family I love. I have nothing to wish for."

"But we owe two hundred dollars to the bank," said Mrs. White.

"Think of handing two hundred dollars to the banker, Papa," said Herbert.

Mr. White stared at the monkey's paw. Then he took a deep breath. "I wish for two hundred dollars."

The next morning, Herbert left for his job at the factory. He wondered how soon his father's wish would come true.

That evening, a man from Herbert's factory came to the door.

"There's been an accident," the man told Mr. and Mrs. White. "Herbert was caught in the machinery at the factory. We couldn't save him. We hope this will help ease your suffering a bit." He handed Mrs. White an envelope.

Mrs. White's hands trembled as she looked inside. "Oh! Oh, no!" she cried.

The packet from Herbert's factory contained two hundred dollars.

"We have two more wishes," said Mrs. White. "We can wish him back. We can have our sweet Herbert back."

"Do you really think that's wise?" said Mr. White. "Do you believe anything good can come from our wishes?"

"Don't you want your son back?" asked Mrs. White.

"Of course I do," said Mr. White. He took out the paw and closed his eyes. "I wish my son Herbert would come back."

Thunder cracked outside the window. Mrs. White heard footsteps outside and flung open the front door. A tall figure stumbled toward her down the road.

Lightning flashed. Mrs. White saw her son clearly. But Herbert was not as he had been that morning.

Mrs. White screamed and slammed the door. "What have we done?" she asked.

"We have one wish left," said Mr. White. "I wish ... I wish my son was dead."

Mrs. White looked out the window. "Our son is gone," she whispered.

"And so are our wishes." Mr. White stared at the shriveled paw in his hands. "Along with our happy life."

He staggered into the parlor and threw the monkey's paw into the fire. And this time Herbert was not there to pull it out.

SWEET MARY

Written by Rebecca Grazulis
Illustrated by Angela Jarecki

Homesville was a nice place. When you walked down the street, someone would always smile and ask how you were doing.

Jack was one of Homesville's citizens. He would spend most of his time playing basketball or baseball with his friends. But he didn't have a friend that he could just talk to.

That's when he met Mary.

It happened quite by accident. Jack was sitting in his car in front of the library when he spotted a girl sitting on the bench across the street. She was wearing a party dress.

"That's the prettiest girl I've ever seen," Jack said. He decided to walk over and introduce himself.

"My name is Jack," he said shyly.

The girl turned to look at Jack. He could see a touch of fear in her eyes.

"Hello," she said softly, "I'm Mary."

Jack saw that Mary was shivering in the cool autumn air, so he gave her his letter jacket. Jack did all of the talking. Mary just smiled and offered a few kind words.

It soon grew dark, so Jack drove Mary home. Before Mary went into the house, she turned, looked at Jack, and smiled. It was the sweetest smile Jack had ever seen.

The next morning, Jack picked a bouquet of flowers and went to Mary's house. A small old woman answered his knock. When Jack asked if he could see Mary, the old woman looked startled.

The old woman looked at Jack carefully. Finally, she said, "Please come in."

The old woman pointed to a picture on the mantel.

"Is this the girl you spoke to?" she asked.

"Yes," replied Jack.

"I am Mrs. Sweet—Mary's mother," she said. "Mary died almost twenty years ago. She's buried in the Homesville Cemetery."

Jack couldn't believe what he was hearing.

Mary Sweet

January 14, 1942-May 5, 1958

Jack ran until he reached the cemetery. He found Mary's tombstone. His letter jacket was draped over it! Jack reached for his jacket and noticed that it smelled faintly of perfume.

"You *did* wear this! You *were* at the bus stop!" he said. "There were so many things I wanted to talk to you about."

Then Mary walked over to Jack and said, "Don't be sad. I'm right here."

Jack could not hear her, but goose bumps rose on his arms at the moment she whispered in his ear.

He didn't know that the sweetest girl he had ever met had come to say good-bye.

A GHOST STORY

Based on the original story by Mark Twain
Adapted by Lisa Harkrader
Illustrated by Ute Simon

I came home from work and eased into my favorite chair. In the newspaper I saw a story about the Cardiff Giant:

STONE MAN HAS PLASTER TWIN

Crowds of people have been lining up to see New York City's own "petrified man" at the Eighteenth Street Exhibit Hall. They believe they are paying to see the stone giant that was discovered on a farm in Cardiff, New York. They don't know that the giant on display at the exhibit hall is merely a plaster cast of the Cardiff Giant.

I laughed. "Some people will believe just about anything." At least now, though, I knew why the street had been so crowded. I lived across from the Eighteenth Street Exhibit Hall.

I closed my eyes and was drifting off to sleep when I heard footsteps in the hallway. The footsteps sounded like boulders being dropped on the floor. With each step, the whole building shook.

Then my blanket slipped off my shoulders. I tugged on it. Something—or someone—tugged harder. I looked up and saw a huge man looming over me.

I screamed. The man screamed.

"You're...you're a ghost," I whispered.

"Yes, and I cannot rest," he replied.

He looked so sad and lost, I forgot to be afraid of him. I scrambled from my bed. The poor giant shivered.

"You must be cold. Sit by the fire," I said.

He stomped over to the fireplace and heaved his body into my favorite chair. The chair shattered beneath him. The giant stood up and looked down at the sticks of wood scattered around him. Then he lumbered over to my bed and sat down. The bed squashed to the floor.

"Stop that!" I yelled. "You'll crush every piece of furniture I own."

I pulled the rug in front of the fire so the giant could sit down. I wrapped a blanket around his shoulders. I set my washtub over his head to keep his ears warm.

The ghost sighed. "I'm so tired. My body is on display for crowds of people. I want to go back to sleep, but I won't be able to rest until they bury my body again."

"You're the Cardiff Giant!" I said.

"The what?" asked the ghost.

I retrieved the newspaper and spread it open to the story about the giant. "Listen to this," I said.

I began reading the story. His eyes grew wide as I read about the plaster imitation.

The ghost stared at me. "The stone man across the street isn't me?"

I shook my head. "He isn't even stone. He's plaster."

"I've been haunting this street for nothing!" cried the ghost.

I reached out to pat his shoulder. "Go to Cardiff. That's where your stone body is."

He lumbered across my apartment and walked out the door. His footsteps thundered across the hall and down the stairs.

I watched the poor ghost of the Cardiff Giant trudge away down the street. Then the ghost turned the corner and disappeared into the darkness.

HAUNTED CEMETERIES

Written by Brian Conway
Illustrated by Jeffrey Ebbeler

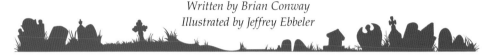

Ghosts and spirits have been seen in many places. But a cemetery is one of the most common places to see a ghost.

Over the years, a lot of strange things have happened at Bachelor's Grove, a cemetery near Chicago. One night, a couple was driving through the cemetery when they saw an old car coming right toward them! They heard screeching brakes and a loud crash. But after the sound of the crash, the old car was nowhere to be found, and their own car did not have a scratch on it.

Woodland Cemetery in Dayton, Ohio, also has almost as many ghosts as graves. One dark night, two college boys decided to take a shortcut through the cemetery.

The boys saw a woman crying on the steps in front of a stone tomb. As they got closer, the boys noticed they could see right through the weeping woman.

When the two students told the cemetery's groundskeeper what they had seen, he nodded. He had heard the story many times before.

"Well," the groundskeeper said, "you're not the first people to meet the Weeping Woman of Woodland."

One famous ghost in Columbus, Ohio, makes so much noise, she wakes up the neighbors! People who live near Camp Chase Cemetery wake up to hear loud cries in the middle of the night.

The sad ghost is known as the Lady in Gray because she wears a gray suit from the 1860's. Some believe she is the wife of Benjamin Allen, a soldier who died at Camp Chase during the Civil War.

One neighbor thought the cries were a loud prank, so he went to investigate. He did not see anyone, but there were footprints in the snow. Then he found two red roses left in front of Benjamin Allen's tombstone.

THE MUMMY

Written by Renee Deshommes
Illustrated by Patrick Browne

Judsen was a famous archaeologist. She had received a map from her friend Rashidi. The map showed Judsen where to find King Elysian's tomb. Judsen and her son Davis were flying to Egypt to meet Rashidi and travel to the tomb together.

"King Elysian was a boy king," Judsen told Davis. "He was ten years old."

"That's how old I am!" said Davis.

"King Elysian became ill soon after he began his reign," Judsen explained. "He died just before he turned eleven."

Finally, the plane touched down in Egypt. As Judsen began gathering the luggage, a man approached her and said, "If you disturb the king's tomb, you will be cursed." Then the man disappeared into the crowd.

"Is that true?" asked Davis.

"King Elysian has been dead for thousands of years," said Judsen. "How could he put a curse on us?"

Just then, their friend Rashidi greeted them. The three explorers went outside and climbed onto their waiting camels. They followed their map, riding across the desert until they came upon the mouth of a cave.

"This is it!" shouted Judsen.

Judsen led the way down into the tomb. The explorers were amazed by all the maps and ancient drawings carved into the walls.

Judsen was backing up to shine her flashlight on the wall. Suddenly, she heard a loud crash.

"Oh, no!" said Judsen. She looked down and found an ancient urn filled with jewels. The jewels had scattered across the ground.

"You must leave everything just as you found it," warned Rashidi.

Judsen and Davis scrambled to pick up the jewels. They did not see that a diamond had rolled into the corner.

"I think we found them all," said Davis.

"Let's find that mummy," said Judsen.

"There it is," whispered Davis.

Judsen's flashlight stopped on a very small mummy. Judsen copied everything she saw down into her notebook.

When it was time to go, Rashidi led the way with his lantern. At the opening of the cave, Judsen stopped and looked up. She saw hieroglyphics above the doorway.

"Rashidi, what do these pictures mean?"

Rashidi held his lantern near the pictures and shook his head. "They are a warning to all visitors," he said. "If anything is disturbed, a curse will follow."

Judsen thought of the urn full of jewels.

The sun was setting in the sky. "We will ride back to my village. You can stay there tonight," Rashidi said.

After a long ride, the three explorers came to a small home made of stone. Davis was so tired that he had fallen asleep on his camel. Judsen helped Davis get down. She carried him inside and put him in bed. She felt Davis's forehead. It was very hot.

"Rashidi," she called, "get a doctor."

The doctor examined Davis, but he could find nothing wrong with the boy.

"This is the curse of King Elysian," he said. "You have disturbed his tomb."

Judsen remembered the jewels in the urn.

"Maybe I didn't pick them all up," she thought. "I must return to the tomb," she whispered.

By daybreak, Judsen was back at the cave. She climbed into the opening and searched the ground for missing jewels.

Suddenly, she noticed something twinkling in a corner of the cavern. It was a sparkling diamond! Judsen quickly returned it to the urn.

Judsen rode back to Rashidi's village. She was relieved, but not surprised, to see that Davis was healthy.

"I'm ready to go on another adventure!" Davis said.

THE TEENY-TINY WOMAN

Adapted by Suzanne Lieurance
Illustrated by Cathy Johnson

Once upon a time there was a teeny-tiny woman who lived in a teeny-tiny house. One day, the teeny-tiny woman decided to go for a teeny-tiny walk. She went a teeny-tiny way before she found a teeny-tiny grave. On top of it was a teeny-tiny bone.

"This teeny-tiny bone will make me some teeny-tiny soup for my teeny-tiny supper," said the teeny-tiny woman. She put the teeny-tiny bone in her teeny-tiny pocket.

Then the teeny-tiny woman walked a teeny-tiny way back to her teeny-tiny house.

The teeny-tiny woman was a teeny-tiny bit tired. She did not feel like making any teeny-tiny soup with the teeny-tiny bone.

The teeny-tiny woman put the teeny-tiny bone into a teeny-tiny jar. Then she put the teeny-tiny jar into her teeny-tiny cupboard.

"I think I will go take a teeny-tiny nap," said the teeny-tiny woman. The teeny-tiny woman crawled into her teeny-tiny bed. Soon the teeny-tiny woman was fast asleep.

The teeny-tiny woman slept for just a teeny-tiny time. Then a teeny-tiny voice woke her. The teeny-tiny voice called out from the teeny-tiny cupboard.

The voice said, "Give me my bone!"

The teeny-tiny woman was a teeny-tiny bit scared. Soon, the teeny-tiny woman went back to sleep. But only for a teeny-tiny time.

The teeny-tiny voice called out again from the teeny-tiny cupboard. This time, the teeny-tiny voice was a teeny-tiny bit louder.

The voice said, "Give me my bone!"

In her loudest, teeny-tiny voice, she said, "TAKE IT!" The teeny-tiny woman went back to sleep and the teeny-tiny voice did not call out from the teeny-tiny cupboard anymore.

The next morning, the teeny-tiny jar and the teeny-tiny bone were gone. The teeny-tiny woman was a teeny-tiny bit hungry again. She hadn't had her teeny-tiny supper.

The teeny-tiny woman went for another teeny-tiny walk. The teeny-tiny woman saw that her teeny-tiny jar was sitting on top of the teeny-tiny marker of the teeny-tiny grave. But the teeny-tiny jar was empty!

Then the teeny-tiny woman saw what looked like a teeny-tiny tooth. She put it in her teeny-tiny jar and walked back to her teeny-tiny house. She put the teeny-tiny jar into her teeny-tiny cupboard.

"Give me my tooth!" said the voice.

This time, the teeny-tiny woman knew just what to do.

In her loudest, teeny-tiny voice, she said, "TAKE IT!"

THE OPEN WINDOW

Based on the original story by Saki
Adapted by Elizabeth Olson
Illustrated by Jennifer Schneider

Vera smiled at Mr. Nuttel. "My aunt will join us soon," said Vera. "You just moved to the country?"

"Yes," said Mr. Nuttel. He fidgeted with his hands. His eye twitched. "I moved here to benefit from country life. Country life is relaxing and slow."

"Do you know anyone in the country?" asked Vera.

"Not a soul," said Mr. Nuttel. "Your aunt, Mrs. Sappleton, is my first new friend. My sister, Olivia, says your aunt is very nice."

"Oh, yes, very nice indeed," said Vera. "She is nice despite the tragedy."

"Tragedy? What do you mean?" asked Mr. Nuttel. His eye twitched. His body shivered.

Vera looked directly into Mr. Nuttel's eyes and said, "Three years ago today, my aunt's husband, two brothers, and their favorite dog left through that window on a hunting trip. They were never seen again."

Mr. Nuttel's eyes widened with fear.

"On the anniversary of their deaths," said Vera, "my poor aunt leaves the window open. She believes that they will return. And, you know, Mr. Nuttel, on such a lovely day as this, I sometimes think they will."

Vera's aunt walked into the room.
"Mr. Nuttel," she said, "I am sorry to keep you waiting. I hope my niece has made you comfortable."

"Y-y-y-es," said Mr. Nuttel.

"I do hope you don't mind the open window," said Mrs. Sappleton. "My husband and brothers are hunting on the moors. They should return soon."

Mr. Nuttel listened with horror. His eye twitched. His body shivered.

"I-I-I see," said Mr. Nuttel, anxious to change the subject. "I moved to the country for the benefit of my nerves. Country life is relaxing and slow, don't you think?"

"Look! Here they are," cried Mrs. Sappleton. "And they're back just in time for tea!" The woman looked out the open window across the green lawn.

Mr. Nuttel could not believe his ears. This poor Mrs. Sappleton needed more help than he did. Mr. Nuttel turned to Vera to show his sympathy, but the child was staring out the window, her eyes wide with horror. Mr. Nuttel turned to look out the window.

Far across the green lawn, a dog ran toward the drawing room. Following the dog was a man with a shotgun resting on his shoulder and two boys carrying sacks.

Mr. Nuttel screamed!

Mr. Nuttel ran out the open window. He ran across the lawn until he disappeared from sight. In his hasty exit, he almost knocked over the returning Mr. Sappleton.

"Such an odd, nervous fellow," Mrs. Sappleton told Mr. Sappleton.

"He was probably frightened by the dog," said Vera. She bent to scratch the dog.

"Makes sense, really," Vera continued. "He told me that he was very scared of dogs. Several years ago a pack of wild dogs chased the poor fellow through the woods for three whole days."

Vera sweetly smiled at her aunt and uncle... Vera liked to tell stories, you see.

DRACULA'S SECRET

Based on the original story by Bram Stoker
Adapted by Elizabeth Olson
Illustrated by Jeremy Tugeau

A galloping horse pulled a coach along a dark road. The driver shouted to his passenger. "Strange things happen around here during the full moon," he said. "Wolves prowl about and bats fill the skies."

Jonathan was carrying a packet with a secret document from London. His boss, Mr. Hawkins, had asked him to deliver the document to Count Dracula of Transylvania.

The coach stopped in front of a dark castle with many towers. As soon as Jonathan climbed down, the coach sped away.

A man in an elegant suit opened the heavy iron door to the castle. "Welcome to Transylvania," said the man. "I've been expecting you."

"Thank you, Count Dracula," said Jonathan. The count's skin was as pale as the full moon. Jonathan heard a wolf howl in the distance. Bats flapped overhead.

"You must be very hungry after your long journey," said the count. He led Jonathan to the dining room.

The count sat down by an empty plate and watched Jonathan eat. "I will eat later," the count said with a smile. Two sharp, white teeth glimmered in the candlelight.

After dinner, Jonathan gave the packet to Count Dracula. "This packet contains a secret document from my boss, Mr. Hawkins."

Dracula smiled widely and took the packet. "Ah, yes," he said. "I have been waiting a long time for this."

The next day, Jonathan decided to explore the long, deserted halls. He followed a twisting staircase deep beneath the castle.

At the bottom, he entered a dark, earthen room lit by torches. Several wooden boxes rested on the floor. Puzzled, Jonathan knelt near one of them. He slowly pulled back the lid. He almost screamed! The box contained Count Dracula. He was a vampire.

Jonathan ran from the room and raced up the staircase. Back in his room, he quickly packed his bag. "I must leave this place at once," he said.

Jonathan ran to the iron door at the castle entrance. He tried to open the door, but it was bolted shut. The count had locked him inside! Jonathan crawled out of a small window and fell to the ground.

Just then a wolf howled in the distance. Bats flew from the castle towers.

Jonathan saw a horse near the castle walls. He jumped on the horse's back. The frightened animal galloped from the castle, carrying Jonathan to safety.

After a very long journey, Jonathan arrived back in London. His wife, Mina, told him that strange things had been happening in London while he was away.

"Bats have been flying over the city," said Mina. "I hear wolves howling."

That night, Jonathan and Mina decided to go to a play. After the play, they walked home along the city streets under the light of a full moon. A man in an elegant suit passed them on the sidewalk.

"Good evening," said the man. The man smiled. Jonathan saw two sharp, white teeth.

Jonathan could not believe his eyes. Count Dracula was in London!

Jonathan walked Mina home. Then he ran to Mr. Hawkins's house.

"Hello, Jonathan," said Mr. Hawkins.

"I must know the meaning of the document I gave to the count," said Jonathan.

"Count Dracula had requested that the document remain secret," said Mr. Hawkins. "But I can tell you now. With that document, he can move to London."

"H-h-he can move here? Count Dracula is going to live in London now?" shouted Jonathan.

"You're going to have a new neighbor," said Mr. Hawkins. "Count Dracula bought the house right next to yours."

FLYING DUTCHMAN

Written by Brian Conway
Illustrated by Daniel Powers

Reid Brenner was the youngest and smallest sailor on the ship. The smallest sailor always had the job of night watch. Reid climbed up the tallest mast to the crow's nest.

Suddenly a fierce storm fell upon the ship. Reid looked down and saw an old ship with tattered sails bobbing on the rough waves. The crew of the strange ship looked up at him. Their faces were pale and gloomy. All their clothes were soaked and torn.

With one last flash of lightning, the storm ended. The ghostly ship was gone.

Sailors tell many stories of the sea. The story of the *Flying Dutchman* has been told for hundreds of years. In 1641, this ship sailed into a terrible storm.

The captain, a proud man named Hendrick Vanderdecken, would not stop or turn his doomed ship around. He ordered his crew to push through the dangerous storm. The *Flying Dutchman* never reached land.

Some sailors say the *Flying Dutchman* still sails the seas today. It is said that the ship must sail through stormy waters forever.

For almost four hundred years, sailors have reported seeing the phantom ship. Usually it is seen at night or during a storm.

The ship's ghostly crew may be seen working on the deck. Some sailors have claimed to see the *Flying Dutchman's* captain. They say he sadly warns them to stay away.

After seeing the phantom ship, many sailors have gotten sick. Some have died not long after reporting a sighting. Any ship that crosses the *Flying Dutchman's* path is said to be doomed, too. Some of those ships have been lost at sea.

The *Flying Dutchman* was a real ship, and it's true that it disappeared during a storm. The terrible tragedies that happened after sightings are also very real. But are the tragedies related to seeing the phantom ship?

HOW HE LEFT THE HOTEL

Based on the original story by Louisa Baldwin
Adapted by Lora Kalkman
Illustrated by Ellen Beier

After the Civil War ended, I headed to
New York City. The city was an exciting
place. I soon found a job at the Empire Hotel.
It was an elegant red brick building.

"We need someone to operate the hotel
elevator from two o'clock in the afternoon
until twelve midnight," said the manager.
"We'll provide wages and a room."

Like everything at the Empire Hotel,
the elevator was modern and fancy. It had
a decorative light inside and mirrors on the
walls. It even had a red velvet sofa.

In November, a new tenant arrived at the Empire Hotel and moved into room 210. His name was Colonel Saxby. Like me, he was also a Civil War veteran. I knew right away because he often wore his military cloak.

Colonel Saxby was a kindly gentleman who kept to himself. He walked with a limp.

"I took a bullet in the knee," he explained to me one day.

Since I worked the elevator, I came to know everyone's routine. Colonel Saxby was especially predictable. He rode the elevator up to the fourth floor at the same time each day. He never rode it down, though. I figured he must have used the stairs.

I was proud to tell people I worked at the Empire Hotel. It was one of New York's finest. Sometimes operating the elevator grew dull, but I really enjoyed all the people.

Every night at midnight, I always locked the elevator. Joe, the doorman, tidied up the lobby a bit. Then, on Wednesdays, we headed to the community room for a game of cards. Helen, one of the hotel housekeepers, often joined us.

One cold February night, Helen brought us an apple pie that she had baked. It was the best I ever tasted. Then Joe began shuffling his well-worn deck of cards. The three of us played until the wee hours of the morning.

The next day, I found myself waiting for Colonel Saxby to arrive. But he never did show up that day. He did not show up the next day either.

"Have you seen Colonel Saxby lately?" I finally asked Joe.

"No," he replied. "I'm told he's very ill."

As the clock struck midnight, the call bell rang on the fourth floor. When I opened the elevator door, I was surprised to see Colonel Saxby. It was the first time I had ever given him a ride down. He looked very ill.

We arrived in the lobby and Joe opened the front door. Colonel Saxby walked out into the snow without saying a word.

Just then, a gentleman with a black bag entered. I could tell at once he was a doctor. He asked to go to the fourth floor. When we arrived there, he rushed straight to room 210.

"I'm too late," I heard the doctor sigh. "I'm afraid Colonel Saxby has passed away."

"That can't be," I said. "Colonel Saxby just left the hotel. Joe saw him, too."

The manager asked me to take Colonel Saxby's body down in the elevator.

"I can't do that, sir," I said. "I can't take the colonel down again."

I knew I couldn't stay at the Empire Hotel any longer—not after what I'd seen. I turned in my keys and left that night.

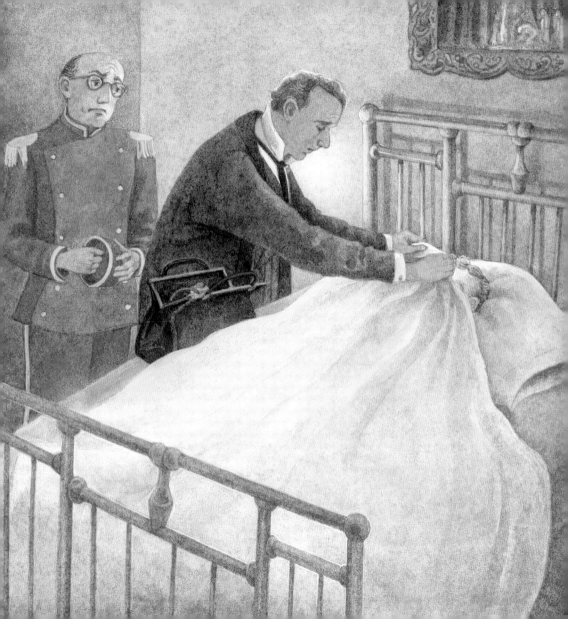

THE RED RIBBON

Adapted by Leslie Lindecker
Illustrated by Gerardo Suzán

Bill knelt down in front of Sally and said,
"Sally, you're the most beautiful girl I've ever
met. I love you and I want you to be my wife.
Will you marry me?"

Sally laughed and said, "Yes! I will."

As Bill gazed lovingly at his bride-to-be,
his eyes lingered on the red velvet ribbon
Sally always wore around her neck.

"Why do you always wear that red
ribbon?" Bill asked.

Sally said, "Bill, I must never take off my
red ribbon!"

Bill and Sally were married that June. Even at the wedding, Sally wore her red ribbon. Bill thought this was odd.

Sally just smiled and said, "I must never take off my red ribbon."

After a few years, Sally found out she was going to have a baby. This news delighted Bill. When the big day came, Sally said, "Please tell the doctor I must not take off my red ribbon!"

Bill was frustrated. He didn't understand why the red ribbon was so important. But he promised Sally that he would tell the doctor. Soon Bill and Sally had a healthy baby boy named Billy.

Bill, Sally, and little Billy lived happily for many years in a small, lovely house in a nice neighborhood.

The red ribbon had frustrated Bill for a long time. Then Bill had an idea. "Our anniversary is coming up. I will buy Sally a beautiful necklace. She will take off that old red ribbon so she can wear the necklace!"

On their anniversary, Bill took Sally to a fancy restaurant. Then Bill gave Sally a velvet box with a beautiful diamond necklace in it. Bill put the necklace around her neck and started to take off the red ribbon.

"I must never take off my red ribbon!" said Sally. Bill sat back in his seat with a huff.

Late that night Bill was still awake. "I've loved Sally for more than twenty years. But she insists on wearing that horrible red ribbon around her neck. I think it's about time I found out why."

Bill got out of bed and walked around to Sally's side. He began to slowly pull on the ends of the bow. The loops of the bow pulled through. Only a half-knot was left. Bill slid his finger under the half-knot and tugged.

ZIP! The red ribbon gave way.

POP! Sally's head came off. It rolled right to the floor, bouncing in the moonlight!

One large tear fell from Sally's eye.

"I warned you!" she said.

DR. JEKYLL'S DIARY

Based on the original story by Robert Louis Stevenson
Adapted by Amy Adair
Illustrated by David Cooper

I am going to write everything down. Mr. Hyde is not far. No, I fear he will come at any moment. I have been in my laboratory just waiting for him.

It all started about a year ago. Back then, I was a good doctor and helped many sick people. But then I invented a magic formula that could make me two different people. My good side would be one person. My bad side would be a totally different person.

In my lab, I poured special powder into a glass. It turned green, then purple, and finally red. Steam rose from the glass. The smell burned my nose. I drank it in one gulp.

I looked in the mirror and gasped! The eyes staring back at me were not Dr. Jekyll's wise brown eyes. The eyes in the mirror were gray and beady. My hair was wild. But I liked the new me. I named this new face Mr. Edward Hyde.

I went out the back door. I climbed into a carriage on the side of the street and yelled, "Take me to Soho!"

I spit out the window. I yelled at people on the street. Oh, how free I felt!

Before I knew it the driver called, "This is Soho, sir."

Instead of paying the driver, I swatted his horse and yelled, "Yah! Away! Yah!" The frightened horse galloped wildly down the street.

Soon it was morning. I hurried home. I sneaked down to my lab and drank my magic formula. I was Dr. Jekyll again.

For months, I was Mr. Hyde by night and Dr. Jekyll by day. One evening, my butler Poole said to me, "Sir, Mr. Utterson is here to see you. He is waiting in the study."

Mr. Utterson looked worried. "Good evening, Dr. Jekyll."

"Good evening," I said. "To what do I owe this visit?"

"Dr. Jekyll, we've been friends for a long time," Mr. Utterson said. "I just wanted to see if anything is wrong."

"Nothing is wrong," I answered.

"You have not been yourself lately," Mr. Utterson said. "This new friend of yours, Mr. Hyde, seems to be trouble. Why would you ever want to be friends with him?"

"Dear Mr. Utterson," I said, "Mr. Hyde may be an interesting character, but I assure you there is nothing to raise concern. Excuse me. I have work to do in my lab."

I went down to the lab and drank my magic formula. This time I only drank half a glass, but I changed into Mr. Hyde even faster. I sneaked out the back door and wandered up and down the streets of London.

When the sun started to rise, I began walking home. Then I accidentally slammed into a little child and knocked her straight to the ground. I yelled, "Get out of my way!"

"Hey, you!" said a stern voice.

I ran away. A police officer chased me.

"You there! Stop!" he yelled, as he grabbed his whistle.

I ran. Faster and faster and faster! If Mr. Hyde went to jail, so would the good Dr. Jekyll. I did not look back. I ran straight to my house and into the lab. I slammed the door. I drank a glass of my magic formula. Nothing happened.

I drank another glass. Still nothing happened. Finally, after four full glasses of the magic formula, I turned back into the good Dr. Jekyll.

I knew that Mr. Hyde could get Dr. Jekyll into trouble. So I locked away my magic formula. It was for the best, because I was running out of the special powder.

But yesterday morning changed everything. I woke with a start. When I looked in the mirror, I saw Mr. Hyde's face. But I had not swallowed any magic formula! Not one single drop! I ran out of my bedroom and down to my lab.

I drank a glass of formula. Nothing happened. After drinking five glasses, I finally changed back into Dr. Jekyll.

An hour later, my head began to ache. I changed into Mr. Hyde once more.

I drank the last six glasses of my magic formula. I don't have any more. I have just a short time left. I am writing so everyone will know the horrible truth that I, Dr. Jekyll, am also **Mr. Hyde.**

I'm just waiting for Mr. Hyde to show his ugly face again. He can come by himself now. He does not need any magic formula. He is much **stronger** than Dr. Jekyll.

I hear **stomp, stomp, stomp, down the steps. The** footsteps are getting closer! **Closer! Closer!** They are just outside my door.

Bang! Bang! Bang! Axes. I hear axes slashing at the door.

Bang! Bang! **They're almost in!**

Mr. Hyde is very near. He'll be here any minute...

THE LOCH NESS MONSTER

Written by Brian Conway
Illustrated by Aaron Boyd

In 1960, a young girl named Alice Logan went sailing on Loch Ness. Loch Ness is a deep lake in Scotland. Alice had heard stories about a sea monster that lived in the lake. People called the creature "Nessie."

Alice leaned over the side of the boat and lost her balance. She fell into the cold water. She saw a huge, swimming beast with a long, thin neck. It had to be Nessie!

Then Alice's life preserver lifted her back to the surface. The strange creature was gone.

Stories about the Loch Ness Monster go back hundreds of years. Altogether, more than four thousand people have reported seeing something unusual in the waters of Loch Ness. The stories are hard to prove because it is so hard to search in the dark lake. Loch Ness is very deep and the water is clouded by tiny floating pieces of brown coal.

Some scientists took photographs in the lake. The photos show an animal that is almost as big as a school bus. The beast has a wide body, fins, a skinny neck, and a tail.

The photographs are real, but many of them are cloudy or unclear. There is still no proof that Nessie exists.

What kind of creature is Nessie? Scientists have many ideas. Some think Nessie could be a type of whale or seal that no one has ever seen before.

Another theory is that Nessie is a relative of a prehistoric fish called the plesiosaur. Scientists always thought the last plesiosaur died millions of years ago. But maybe Nessie's relatives have lived in the lake for all these years.

Is it possible that Nessie and all of her relatives have lived in Loch Ness for millions of years? If the creature exists, it knows how to hide well. Will Nessie and her family members ever reveal themselves to us?

THE LIGHTHOUSE

Written by Renee Deshommes
Illustrated by Laurie Harden

Jack was a writer who moved to a seaside town. He traveled the coast to write stories about the people there. He didn't know that he would soon have his own story to tell.

After settling into his new home by the sea, Jack decided that he needed some artwork. At a local gallery, he found a painting of a lighthouse. It reminded him of the lighthouse at the edge of town.

Jack walked home with the painting under his arm. He could not wait to find the perfect place to hang it.

That afternoon, Jack found a place above his mantel. He hammered a nail into the wall and hung the picture.

That evening, Jack thought he saw shadows moving across the dark room. Then he caught a glimpse of a ghostly old man.

"Perhaps I'm just tired," he thought. "My eyes must be playing tricks on me." Jack turned out the light and went to bed.

That night, he dreamed about the lighthouse in his new painting. Jack was standing on its platform. He saw an old man sitting alone inside the lighthouse.

The man seemed very sad. Jack tried to speak to him. Then Jack woke up.

The next morning, Jack felt like he had to move the painting. He looked around his house for the perfect place. He decided the best place for the painting was right above his desk in the den.

That evening, Jack sat down at his desk to work. He was reading a book about lighthouses when a strange feeling came over him. He felt very cold.

Then in the corner, Jack saw the shadow again. This time, Jack was sure it was an old man. The man seemed sad and restless.

Jack was very puzzled. He began thinking about the painting. "Could that be why the shadow is here?" he wondered.

That night, Jack had a dream that the old man was looking out the window of the lighthouse. He was staring at the sea and the gulls. The old man looked so happy!

The next day, Jack found the perfect place for the painting. It was directly across from his biggest window. Jack carefully hung the painting. Then he turned around to look at the sea. "Yes!" he exclaimed. "This is definitely the perfect place."

That night, Jack waited for the ghostly shadow to appear. But it never did. Jack noticed that a certain sense of peace had come over his house. He stopped dreaming about the old man in the lighthouse, too.

Soon after the strange shadow had disappeared, Jack started working on a new project. He was writing a story about the painting and the ghostly shadow.

Jack decided to take a break from his writing. He got up from his desk and walked over to the painting.

Jack grabbed a cloth and dusted the wooden frame. Then he stopped to look at the picture. Jack noticed something he had never seen before. A man was standing on the platform of the lighthouse. He was looking out to sea.

Then Jack realized that it was the same man that he had seen in his dreams!

NIGHT COACH

Based on the original story by Amelia Edwards
Adapted by Lora Kalkman
Illustrated by Jeffrey Ebbeler

Orange kicked the dusty, dry dirt with the toe of his leather boot. He had been on his way to see his brother Pete. But now he was stranded in the desert.

"Musta been a rattler," Orange thought. Whatever it was, it sure scared his horse Gypsy. She had reared up and flung Orange from her back. By now, she was long gone.

Much to his surprise, Orange spotted a tiny cabin. A small trail of smoke rose from the chimney. He knew that the desert got very cold at night, so he started walking.

It was plenty dark when Orange finally made it to the cabin. But he could still see the dim light inside. He rapped at the door.

An old man, stout and balding, opened the door a crack. "Can I help you?" he asked cautiously.

"Why, yes, sir. I hope so, sir," Orange said. "Seems my horse got spooked and left me stranded here. I was hopin' you might give me shelter for the night."

"It's not too late to catch the night coach into town," the man offered. "You just need to walk out to Red Rock Hollow." The old man showed Orange on a map. "It's the most direct route through the valley."

Orange thanked the old man for the suggestion and set off.

The desert felt much colder by the time Orange saw Red Rock Hollow before him. Suddenly, he noticed two tiny, dim lights shining through the hollow. Orange realized it must be the night coach.

Now, Orange had seen a lot of coaches in his day, but he had never seen one like this! It was black from top to bottom. A jet black horse wearing a giant black plume pulled it. The driver, who had not said a word, was draped in a heavy black cloak.

"Well, this is mighty strange," Orange thought. But he hopped inside anyway.

Before long, the black horse was galloping at full speed. Its hooves thundered across the desert floor. Orange wondered why the driver was going so fast. He decided he better say something. He leaned right out the window.

"Evenin', my good man," he shouted. "I thank you kindly for the ride. How long will it take us to get to town? It shouldn't take too long at this pace."

He waited for the reply, but the driver said nothing. He was relieved when the driver finally turned around. But relief soon turned to horror. The driver had no face!

Orange's eyes grew wide. Out of sheer terror, he closed his eyes and jumped.

When Orange woke up, he discovered he was in a bed. His brother, Pete, was there, as well as Pete's wife and a doctor.

"Orange!" Pete said. "We're gonna have to change your name. Your hair done turned pure white! Like you seen a ghost."

Orange began to shudder. It was all coming back to him now. He could still see the black coach and the black horse.

"Don't you worry none," said Pete as he patted Orange's shoulder. "We've arranged to have a coach take you on home."

"No! No coaches!" Orange blurted out. "A horse'll suit me fine, Pete. Just make sure it's not black."

HOUDINI'S GREAT ESCAPE

Written by Brian Conway
Illustrated by Allan Eitzen

Harry Houdini was probably the most famous magician of all time. People especially loved Houdini's great escape tricks. But his most famous trick was one he did after he was already dead!

Houdini promised his wife, Bess, that he would contact her from beyond the grave. With his last breaths, Houdini whispered a secret message to Bess. This way, she would know it was really Harry speaking to her from beyond the grave.

On Halloween, 1926, Harry Houdini died.

Bess always kept a candle burning near a picture of her husband. Each year she held a séance on Halloween. A séance is when a group of living people try to talk to the spirits of people who have died.

In 1929, a man named Arthur Ford came to the séance on Halloween. He closed his eyes and began to whisper and hum. His voice changed suddenly.

"Hello, Bess," Ford said in a very strange voice. The voice sounded just like Harry's. A cold breeze came through the open window and blew out a nearby candle. The table shook. Then Ford slowly repeated the secret code. Bess was amazed!

Did Houdini really figure out a way to speak to his wife from the spirit world? Or was the séance a hoax?

One newspaper article said Bess Houdini and Arthur Ford made a deal. If she told him Harry Houdini's secret message, he would share some of his riches with her. In fact, Ford became quite famous after the séance.

Other people believed, and still believe, that Harry's spirit really did speak to Bess. Even today, people hold séances on Halloween night every year. They try to talk to Houdini. They believe that if anyone could have escaped death, it would be Harry Houdini, the greatest escape artist of all time.

THE SELKIE CHILD

Written by Amy Adair
Illustrated by Beatriz Helena Ramos

Martin tied his fishing boat to the dock and began to walk home. Near the shore, he noticed a small bundle next to a seal skin.

"This must be a Selkie baby," whispered Martin. He had heard fishermen tell tales about Selkies that could change from seals to humans by shedding their skins.

Martin brought the baby home to his wife Sela. "Let's name her Morgan," Martin said.

Martin did not tell Sela that Morgan was a Selkie child. Instead, he locked the baby's little seal skin in a trunk in the attic.

226

Morgan grew up to be a beautiful child. Sela and Morgan would spend the days swimming while Martin fished.

One day, a big storm blew up the coast while Martin was fishing. He never came home. The next morning, pieces of Martin's boat washed up on the beach.

Late that night, Sela went to check on Morgan. She was shocked to find the bed empty! She looked out the window and saw Morgan standing on the rocks. Sela walked down to the water to bring Morgan home.

"Mama," Morgan said. "Do you ever feel like you don't belong here?"

"No," said Sela. "I belong here with you."

When Sela and Morgan got back to the house, they heard *stomp, stomp, stomp* above their heads.

"Someone is upstairs," Sela gasped.

Creeaakk! The attic door was opening.

Sela lit a candle and tiptoed up the steps. Morgan followed close behind.

Sela peeked inside the attic. A trunk suddenly slid toward her. Sela reached down and opened it. She felt something cold and wet inside the trunk. It was a tiny seal's skin!

"Come with me!" Sela said. She grabbed Morgan's trembling hand and led her down three flights of steps to the basement. Sela opened a large chest.

"I hid this here years ago," Sela explained. She pulled out a seal's skin.

"What is it?" Morgan whispered.

"It's a seal's skin," Sela answered. "I've never told anyone that I'm a Selkie."

Sela showed Morgan the smaller skin. "Your father must have known you were a Selkie. He just didn't know how to tell me."

Sela and Morgan ran to the beach and slipped into their seal skins. As they swam, they saw a familiar boat drifting along.

Sela looked up and saw the ghostly figure of her husband standing on the boat's deck. A wave splashed over Sela and Morgan. They blinked their eyes and the boat was gone.

GHOST CAVE

Written by Lisa Harkrader
Illustrated by Kathleen Estes

Riley was the foreman of a road construction crew. One morning, a teenage boy showed up at the work site.

"My name's Tate," he said. "I'm here for the job. I can do the work of three men."

Tate grasped the bumper of Riley's truck with one hand. He took a deep breath and lifted the front of the truck off the ground.

Riley laughed. "Okay, you've got the job."

Tate worked hard every day. He never took a break. At the end of each day, Tate took his pay and walked toward town.

On Saturday, Riley went into town for a haircut and a shave.

"I've got a new worker on the crew," Riley told the barber. "He can't be more than fifteen or sixteen. His name's Tate."

"I know Tate," said the barber. "But he has to be at least twenty. Lived here all his life. But the funny thing is, he doesn't seem to get any older. He's even worn the same clothes for the last five years, and he never needs a haircut."

Riley frowned. "That's very strange. Think I should have a talk with him?"

"No," said the barber. "He's a good boy. His mama's sickly, and she needs him."

As Riley left the barbershop, he saw Mrs. Malloy and Mrs. Winslow chatting in front of the dress shop.

"Poor Tate," said Mrs. Malloy.

"Tate?" Riley wheeled around. "Pardon me. I don't mean to eavesdrop, but were you just talking about a boy named Tate?"

"Yes. His mother passed away this morning," said Mrs. Malloy.

"She's been sick for a very long time," said Mrs. Winslow.

Mrs. Malloy nodded. "He spent all his time caring for her. It's as if he had no other purpose in life. I don't know what will become of the poor boy now."

Suddenly, Mrs. Malloy's son came running up.

"Mama, Mama!" the boy cried. "We were playing near the creek and Tate walked by. I could see right through him."

"Don't make up stories," said Mrs. Malloy.

"I'm not!" said Jimmy. "We followed him out past the old mill and he walked into a cave. He got paler and paler until he just disappeared. I've got to catch up with the other kids. They went to tell the sheriff." Jimmy raced down the street.

Riley laughed. "He has an active imagination. Tate is certainly pale, but I don't think he could actually disappear."

On Monday morning, Tate did not come to work. Riley remembered Jimmy's story and set out down the road past the old mill.

When he got to the cave, Riley saw that the sheriff had gotten there before him. In the middle of the cave, Riley saw Tate's clothes and work boots rotting in a heap around a brittle skeleton.

"I'd say this skeleton has been here about five years," said the sheriff. "I found this in his pocket. It's his mother's grocery bill."

Riley pointed to the date on the paper. Tate had paid the bill on Saturday, the very day his mother died. "I guess he can stop taking care of his mother now," said Riley.

INTERVIEW WITH DR. FRANKENSTEIN

Based on the original story by Mary Shelley
Adapted by Brian Conway
Illustrated by Fabricio Vanden Broeck

One day, Henry Clerval went to visit his old friend Dr. Victor Frankenstein. Clerval asked the doctor many questions about his latest experiment.

Dr. Frankenstein explained how he had tried to create a living man. Instead, he had created a monster. Dr. Frankenstein was so frightened by his monster that he ran away from his lab. When he returned the next day, the monster was gone.

Dr. Frankenstein looked everywhere for the monster. As he searched, he talked to many people who had seen the creature.

One man saw the monster in the woods near the laboratory. The monster had seen the man's campfire and been attracted to the light and warmth of the fire. The man was frightened by the monster. He ran to the village and told everyone what he saw.

The villagers went back to the woods with torches and clubs. They were afraid of the monster. They did not know that the monster was also afraid of them.

The frightened monster ran away from the village and into the countryside.

"The monster hid in a cave so that no one would see him," said Dr. Frankenstein. "But he grew very lonely."

"What did he do next?" asked Clerval.

"He discovered a cottage not far from his cave," replied Dr. Frankenstein. "An old blind man lived in the cottage with his two children. The monster would watch them through the window. The monster loved to hear their voices. He also loved the sweet sound of the old man's guitar."

"Did the family ever discover the monster by their home?" asked Clerval.

"Yes, they did," said Dr. Frankenstein. "That was when his happiness ended."

"How did they find him?" Clerval asked.

The doctor explained that one day the blind man was home alone. The monster approached the blind man and they talked for a long time.

Then the children returned. Since their father was blind, he could not see the terrifying creature beside him. But the poor children could see the hideous monster. They were afraid. They screamed and shouted.

The creature tried to wave his arms to tell the children not to be afraid. The boy grabbed a log from the fire and swung it at the monster. The frightened monster gave up and ran away.

"What happened next?" Clerval asked.

"I was still looking for the monster," Dr. Frankenstein said. "He sounded like he was kind and gentle. I wanted to give him a safe place to live."

"Did you ever find him?" Clerval asked.

"No," answered Dr. Frankenstein. "I heard many stories about the monster. Everyone was scared of him. The monster ran farther and farther away from people."

Dr. Frankenstein explained how he followed the monster all the way to the North Pole. It was a vast land covered with ice and snow. Dr. Frankenstein searched there for the monster, but he could not find him.

"What have I done?" Dr. Frankenstein shook his head and cried. "I gave the monster life, but it is a terrible life."

"Do you think the monster is angry with you?" Clerval asked.

"The monster must be lonely and angry," Dr. Frankenstein said.

Clerval shook his head sadly. "Then, my friend, it is good that you never found the monster. He might be looking for revenge."

"I doubt that I will ever see the monster again," said Dr. Frankenstein.

Just then, a bolt of lightning struck.

"It's good to be home," he continued, "where I'll be comfortable and safe again."

BIGFOOT

Written by Brian Conway
Illustrated by Jason Wolff

One summer in 1966, Tim and Tanya Saunders went camping. They were playing near their campsite when they saw something move in the trees.

Just then, a giant, furry creature stepped out from behind a large tree. It stood on two feet like a human being. It looked at them curiously with its big, black eyes.

Tim and Tanya screamed and ran as fast as they could. When they returned with their mom and dad, the creature was gone. All that was left was a single footprint.

What Tim and Tanya saw in the woods is called a Bigfoot. Nearly two thousand people have told stories like Tim and Tanya's. All of these people saw a furry giant that stood up like a human and walked on two feet.

Many Bigfoot tracks have been found in the woods. The footprints look like human footprints, but are much larger and deeper. Scientists say that any creature that could make footprints like that would be eight feet tall and weigh eight hundred pounds!

Some people have gone into the woods to find a real Bigfoot and photograph it. Experts who look at their photos cannot tell if the creatures in the photos are real or fake.

In 1967, Robert Patterson brought a movie camera to the woods. His famous film shows a female Bigfoot who is about seven feet tall and weighs about three hundred pounds. His film is the best evidence of a Bigfoot, but some people think the Bigfoot in the movie is a man wearing a furry costume.

Many scientists say the photos and the footprints are not strong enough proof. They want to see bones or even a real Bigfoot! Until then, they will think Bigfoot is a myth.

Bigfoot stories are very real to people who have seen these creatures. Tim and Tanya Saunders will never forget that summer day when they saw Bigfoot in the woods.

THE WRECKERS' DAUGHTER

Written by Virginia R. Biles
Illustrated by Teresa Flavin

Chambercombe Manor is a very large
house on the rocky coastline of Devonshire,
England. One owner after another has
reported seeing the ghost of a young woman.
But no one ever knew who she was—not for
three hundred long years.

Then about one hundred years ago, the
owner of the house discovered a tiny room
hidden behind plastered walls. Inside the
little room was the skeleton of a young
woman. She was lying on a beautiful bed.
Who was she? Why was she there?

In the 1600's, Chambercombe Manor was owned by Thomas and Mary Oatway. The Oatways owned a little shop. But no one knew that the Oatways were wreckers.

During stormy weather, when the Oatways knew that a ship was sailing past the coastline, they would build a fire on the shore. The captain of the ship would think the fire was a light to guide him to safety. He would sail into the big rocks on the coast.

The ship would crash into pieces and the cargo would wash up on the shore. The Oatways would gather all the valuable goods and sell them in their store. No passengers or crew ever lived to tell the story.

One stormy night long ago, lightning flashed and Thomas saw a ship on the sea.

Mary and Thomas built a blazing fire and waited. At last they heard the crunch of wood as the bow of the ship struck the rocks.

"It's wrecked," Thomas yelled.

As they began to search for boxes and crates, the yellow rays from their lantern fell on a still body lying in the sand. The woman's face had cuts from the jagged rocks.

"There's a woman here," Thomas called. "She's injured, but she's still breathing."

"We can't leave her here," replied Mary.

Thomas picked up the woman and carried her to their house.

They put the woman in Elizabeth's bedroom. Elizabeth was their daughter. Thirteen years ago, the young girl had run away in search of adventure. Mary and Thomas missed their daughter very much.

Mary sat by the injured woman on the bed. She had cleaned her face and wrapped bandages around it. There was nothing else she could do. Mary stayed at the bedside until the young woman stopped breathing.

Thomas and Mary feared that if they reported the death, everyone would know they were wreckers. They decided to hide the body. They moved the woman's body to a small room and plastered over the doorway.

Three days passed. Mary was pouring the tea when she heard a knock at the front door. She opened the door. Before her stood a tall, well-dressed man. His head was bandaged. His arm was in a sling.

Mary and Thomas offered the man tea and listened nervously as he began to speak.

"Four days ago, I was on a ship from Ireland. The ship sank off your coast. I am the only survivor," he said. "I met your daughter, Elizabeth, on the ship. She told me she had run away to Ireland and married a wealthy Irish gentleman. She missed you terribly and was coming to visit. It was supposed to be a surprise."

In the 1960's, construction workers were tearing down an old house in Ireland. They found a metal box. It held a letter addressed to the owners of Chambercombe Manor.

My wife and I lived for a number of years in Chambercombe Manor. We were blessed with a beautiful daughter, who ran away when she was still a girl. We caused a ship to wreck, and the wreck killed our own daughter. We placed her body in a secret room. We could no longer live in our house. We thought we saw our daughter's ghost in the house. We moved to Ireland so we could be near our grandchildren.

May God forgive us.

Signed, Thomas Oatway

1690

THE INN AT THE END OF THE LANE

Written by Lora Kalkman
Illustrated by Teri Weidner

Erica and her mother were going on vacation. Mom had made plans for them to stay with Aunt Jill. Aunt Jill lived in a quaint little town near the ocean.

The sky was a bit overcast as Erica and her mother turned onto the interstate. As they headed north, it started to rain furiously. There was a loud crack of thunder. A bolt of lightning lit up the sky. It was raining so hard that they could barely see the road.

"Look," Mom said, leaning forward and squinting. "There's an inn up ahead."

Erica felt relieved as they pulled up to a big, white farmhouse. Erica and her mother grabbed their suitcases and rushed to the front porch. Thankfully, the porch was covered, providing shelter from the rain. Mom rang the doorbell.

"Welcome," said the innkeeper, as she opened the door. "Please come in."

"We'd like a room," said Erica's mother.

"Certainly, dear," the lady said.

The lady led the travelers to a cozy upstairs bedroom. Erica could hardly wait to climb in bed under the warm, dry cover

In the morning, Erica and her mother went downstairs. They could not find the innkeeper anywhere.

Erica's mother shrugged her shoulders. "Maybe she went out for groceries," she said. "We can just leave a note."

Erica's mother wrote a short note and left it on the hall table along with some money.

After driving a few miles, they stopped at a gas station. Erica's mother asked the man working there to fill the tank.

"That sure was a terrible storm last night," Erica's mother continued. "Fortunately, we were able to spend the night at that charming inn a few miles back."

The man looked puzzled. "That's Mrs. Flattery's old inn," the man said. "It burned down several years ago."

Erica's mother thought the man was joking. But Erica had a creepy feeling.

"Let's drive back, Mom," she suggested. "It will only take a few minutes."

Erica held her breath as they approached the inn. Sure enough, the old house was burned, just like the man had said.

The porch was sagging and the windows were all broken. Erica made her way to the opening where the front door used to be. She gasped! There before her on the hall table was their money and neatly folded note.

THE BANSHEE AND O'DOUD

Written by Lynne Suesse
Illustrated by Frank Sofo

Aiken O'Doud was a man of few beliefs. He did not believe in leprechauns or fairies. The only thing Aiken O'Doud believed was that he knew everything.

O'Doud was a reporter for a newspaper. His boss would send him to different places to write stories. One day his boss told him to go to the Irish village of Limerick to write a story about the banshee.

O'Doud packed his bag and bought a train ticket. "I will write the story, but I will not believe in banshees," he grumbled.

O'Doud grumbled to himself as he rode the train. "Banshees? Ha!" he muttered.

O'Doud arrived at the Cloverleaf Inn. He got right to work and began to ask questions about the banshee. The innkeeper told O'Doud how the banshee took the life of an old woman on the edge of the village.

"How do you know that the banshee had anything to do with it?" asked O'Doud.

The innkeeper told O'Doud the villagers had heard screaming. "It was the howling of the banshee!" cried the innkeeper. "We all heard it just before the old woman fell."

"I don't believe such a thing," said O'Doud. "It must have been the wind."

Next O'Doud went to interview the old woman's neighbors at the edge of the village.

Timmy O'Daley lived next door to the old woman's house. Timmy told O'Doud about the screaming he had heard the day the old woman disappeared.

"It was probably just the wind howling," grumbled O'Doud.

Timmy ignored O'Doud and went on to tell him about the legend of the banshee.

"Nobody sees her," Timmy explained. "You know she is coming when you hear her scream. But her victim never hears the scream. So if everyone around you hears screaming and you don't, you're in trouble."

O'Doud walked back into the village. He knew he needed some more information so he could write his newspaper story.

O'Doud stopped to talk to Minnie O'Connell. Minnie ran the bakery. She was talking to Mrs. O'Malley.

"The banshee does not like those who don't believe," Mrs. O'Malley said.

"How do you know the banshee is real?" O'Doud asked.

"The likes of you better be careful," warned Minnie.

O'Doud thought the women were trying to scare him. It did not work. O'Doud went back to the Cloverleaf Inn to sleep.

The next morning, O'Doud did not want to talk to more villagers. He thought the people in the village did not like him. He did not care. He thought that they were silly people with silly beliefs.

O'Doud found a restaurant near the inn. He ordered breakfast and a cup of coffee.

"Did you hear the screaming last night?" the waiter asked O'Doud.

O'Doud sipped his coffee, then shook his head. He had not heard any screaming.

"It kept me up," said the waiter. "It sounded just like the screaming I heard right before the old woman disappeared."

"I'm sure it was the wind," said O'Doud.

O'Doud paid for his meal and left the restaurant. He wondered why he had not heard all the noise during the night.

As he walked near the village square, O'Doud looked at all the people. They had strange looks on their faces. He saw people covering their ears, as if they heard a loud sound. But O'Doud did not hear anything. O'Doud felt dizzy. He could not breathe.

Suddenly, O'Doud was struck down by the banshee! The people of Limerick gathered around the man who had doubted.

Then a leprechaun peeked from behind a stone and said, "Is the doubter gone, then?"

Indeed, he was.

THE SECOND CAPTAIN

Written by Lisa Harkrader
Illustrated by Jo Ellen Bosson

Robert and the captain stood on the pier, watching their crew load the remaining crates into the hull of the long freighter. Icy wind whipped in from the ocean. Robert huddled down in his jacket.

Robert was the ship's first mate, the captain's right-hand man. But this was his first trip to Newfoundland.

"We'll have to remain alert," warned Captain Connor. "Our ship is sturdy, but it would shatter against an iceberg. You'll need to be ready for icebergs."

Robert and Captain Connor boarded the ship. The captain recorded their departure in the ship's logbook while Robert began his navigational calculations.

After about an hour, the captain stood up. "Robert, I need to go below to chart the ship's position," he said.

The ship was far out at sea. Their best helmsman, O'Brien, was at the wheel.

Robert set back to work and finished his calculations. When he looked up, he was startled to see Captain Connor at his desk, scrawling in the ship's logbook.

"Captain?" said Robert.

The captain did not answer.

Robert rubbed his eyes. The captain's desk was empty. The captain was gone.

"That's odd." Robert frowned. "The captain didn't say a word. He must be worried about something."

Robert walked over to the captain's desk. The logbook was still open. Robert read the latest entry:

Change position immediately.
Tack northwest ten degrees.

Robert stared at the captain's words. "That changes our course completely. Why didn't he say something?" He turned to the helmsman. "Tack northwest ten degrees. Immediately. I'll go find the captain."

Robert searched everywhere. He finally found the captain in the infirmary. A bandage covered the captain's head.

"Captain!" cried Robert. "I saw the note you wrote when you returned to your desk. I changed course as you requested."

The captain stared at Robert. "I didn't return to my desk. I hit my head when I was climbing down the ladder to the chart room."

Now it was Robert's turn to stare. "Sir, I can show you the note. I'll be right back."

When Robert returned to get the ship's logbook, he saw O'Brien leaning on the wheel. He was steering away from a huge iceberg close to the port side of the ship.

"If we didn't change course when we did, we would've hit it head-on," said O'Brien.

Robert snatched the ship's logbook from the captain's desk and hurried back down to the infirmary.

The captain studied the book. "It's my handwriting, but I never wrote this!"

The captain sat straight up in bed. "My dream! In my dream I saw an iceberg. I knew we were going to hit it. I tried to tell you, but I just could not get your attention."

"Captain, in your dream, what did you do next?" asked Robert.

The captain's face went white. "I wrote 'tack northwest ten degrees' in the logbook."

THE LITTLE ROOM

Written by Leslie Lindecker
Illustrated by Nan Brooks

Maria and her sister Claudia were riding
the train to their aunts' house. They had not
visited the house since childhood. But they
both remembered the secret room.

"Did you ever open the door to the secret
room?" asked Claudia.

"Yes," said Maria. "The room was filled
with sunshine. The furniture was brightly
painted. There were seashells everywhere."

"Did you go inside?" Claudia asked.

"I tried," said Maria. "But Aunt Bedelia
chased me away from the door."

"I saw the room once," said Claudia. "It wasn't at all like you remember it. The room was cool and dark. The walls were covered with beautiful wallpaper. There were vases of roses everywhere."

"Did you go inside?" Maria asked.

"I tried," said Claudia. "But Aunt Magnolia chased me away from the door."

"Isn't it strange that we remember the room so differently?" asked Maria.

"It's quite a mystery," Claudia answered.

"It will be good to see Aunt Bedelia and Aunt Magnolia again," Maria said.

"Yes, it will," replied Claudia. "I just hope they will finally let us see the secret room."

As soon as Maria and Claudia arrived, they asked their aunts about the room.

"Both of us remember a secret room in your house," said Maria. "I remember seeing sunshine and seashells in the room, but Claudia remembers shadows and roses."

"The room you remember does not have shells in it," said Aunt Bedelia. "Nor does it have roses in it. Come and have a look."

The two young ladies followed their aunts to the room. When the door opened, Claudia and Maria saw a cellar with a dirt floor. In the center, a stone marker read:

Shelly and Rose
December 31, 1948

"One winter night," Aunt Bedelia began, "there was a terrible snowstorm. We heard a knock at the door. It was a young woman with a baby. They were freezing cold. We did our best to take care of them that night. When morning came, both the baby and the young woman had died in their sleep."

Aunt Magnolia continued the story. "It was winter and the ground outside was frozen. We had to bury them in the cellar. The young woman had left a note that said, 'Take care of my Rose — Shelly.'"

"Some days this is just our cellar," said Aunt Bedelia. "On other days, it is a room filled with roses or seashells."

"We never could find anyone who knew the young woman," said Aunt Magnolia. "But I think she knew we tried to help her. Whenever the room appears, there is a happy feeling in it."

Maria, Claudia, Aunt Bedelia, and Aunt Magnolia walked back up the stairs. As the young women and their aunts stepped back into the kitchen, the cellar began to fade.

If they had looked back, they would have seen that the room was bright and sunny. There were many seashells scattered about. There were vases full of roses on the tabletops. A young woman sat in a rocking chair and sang softly to a sweet little baby.

GHOST HUNTERS

Written by Brian Conway
Illustrated by Cheryl Kirk Noll

Friday night used to be the busiest night at Jim's Village Inn. But now very few people came to Jim's restaurant. People said that it was haunted.

One Friday night, some new customers came in for dinner. As Jim watched, their table shook and their drinks crashed to the floor. The shocked family wanted an explanation. But Jim did not have one.

Jim picked up the phone and called Incident Investigations. That night, the company sent a ghost hunter to investigate.

Ghost hunters work at night. They study poltergeists. Poltergeists are ghosts that knock things over and make a lot of noise. A ghost hunter's tool kit might contain a camera, a sound recorder, and a thermometer.

Harry Price was a famous ghost hunter. He studied hundreds of haunted places. He did not believe a place was haunted until he could find scientific proof. He would record sounds and watch for movement.

Sometimes tables shook, lamps fell over, or doors locked. There was nobody in the houses but Harry Price, and he had not moved. These were places that Harry Price proved were haunted.

Other famous ghost hunters were some of history's most respected scientists. Sir William Crookes studied haunted houses in England during the 1800's. He attended many séances, where people got together to try to talk to spirits. He saw and heard many things that science could not explain.

Today's ghost hunters have advanced machines that can sense the slightest changes in temperature or movements in the air.

A ghost hunter proved that Jim's Village Inn was inhabited by mischievous spirits. It is now called Jim's Haunted Inn. Every Friday night, people come from miles around to dine in the presence of a poltergeist.

THE END